Have You Been to the Beach Lately?

poems by
Ralph Fletcher

photographs by
Andrea Sperling

Orchard Books
New York

*An Imprint of
Scholastic Inc.*

for Mom—
you held my hand
when I trembled
on the shore

Text copyright © 2001 by Ralph Fletcher
Photographs copyright © 2001 by Andrea Sperling

Orchard Books, an imprint of Scholastic Inc.
95 Madison Avenue, New York, NY 10016

Manufactured in the United States of America
Book design by Mina Greenstein
The text of this book is set in 12 point Optima.
The illustrations are black-and-white photographs.

10 9 8 7 6 5 4 3 2 1

Library of Congress Cataloging-in-Publication Data
Fletcher, Ralph J.
Have you been to the beach lately?: poems / by Ralph Fletcher ;
photographs by Andrea Sperling.
     p.   cm.
ISBN 0-531-30330-6 (alk. paper)
1. Beaches—Juvenile poetry. 2. Seaside resorts—Juvenile poetry.
3. Children's poetry, American. [1. Beaches—Poetry. 2. American
poetry.] I. Sperling, Andrea, ill. II. Title.
PS3556.L523 H38 2001 811'.54—dc21 00-61130

Contents

Have You
Been to the
Beach Lately?

≈ The First Time

On my first trip to the beach
the sea refused to cooperate.

It kept curling and whirling
      bobbing and weaving
      clearing its throat
      whenever a wave drew back.

It kept moving and grooving
      shucking and jiving
      dishing and dancing
      razzling and dazzling

wouldn't keep still even
long enough to shake hands.

≈ Soul Talk

My little brother Ben
heard the word *soul* at church
and now he's obsessed.
That's all he talks about.

> *Does Santa Claus*
> *have a soul, Mom?*

> *Could my soul count*
> *every speck of sand*
> *on this beach?*

Mom says: *I don't know.*
Now hold still so I can put
sunscreen on your back.

> Ben tells her:
> *Well, put on lots so I*
> *don't get soul-burned.*

≈ Peace

Nobody argues around here.
Nobody fights. The beach
calms people down.

Strangers say hi, offer food.
Kids share their sand toys
with kids they don't even know.

A guy gets whacked on the head
by a Frisbee I throw
and he doesn't even yell at me.

The only squawking
comes from two seagulls
arguing over a slice of bread.

This place makes me think of those rocks
tumbling around in the shallow surf,
sharp edges all worn smooth.

≈ Bodies

You can't hide very much
when you're only wearing
a bathing suit.

That man over there must have
the hairiest chest
on earth.

That tall woman is really pretty
even with the cobra tattoos
on her back.

See the thick arms
on that short guy?
He sort of looks
like Popeye.

That huge woman has legs
like mounds of jiggly Jell-O

      but here at the beach
      no one seems to care.

≋Getting Buried

The beach is no place for worrying
but my brain starts churning:

> summer school
> getting better grades
> football tryouts
> four weeks away

I let Ben bury me in the sand:
my legs, belly, chest, arms,
'til only my head is sticking out
like a lost lumpy basketball.

For a while he torments me,
then gets bored and runs off.
I sit back in cool sand,
eyes closed, snug as a crab.

Amazing how light I feel,
weightless and carefree,
this heavy blanket
piled high on top of me.

≋ Tsunami

I love watching the breaking surf
but there's one wave I never want to see

Imagine: a freak tide so swift
you actually see the sea retreating,

an ominous draining of seawater
like a plug pulled on the ocean floor

Tidal pools appear offshore where
no one has ever seen them before

You see huge rocks, exposed wrecks,
trapped fish flopping on wet sand

A hush, a beachy stillness. Then:
a faint roar that slowly grows louder

A new horizon: a monstrous wave
ugly with debris pulled off the sea floor,

a hundred feet high/ten billion tons/
brute force/pure destruction/unstoppable

≈Gullible

Ben digs up a clam,
skinny and sharp,
and asks if it's a razor clam.

That's a laser clam, I tell him.
It shoots lasers at bad guys,
and he believes me.

He finds a chunk of a sand dollar,
a quarter piece,
And asks what that's worth.

Exactly twenty-five cents,
I tell him,
and he believes that too.

≈ The Lifeguard

Like a god
on Mount Olympus
he sits far above
the common people.

Like an arrogant god
with a perfect body
he tosses down smiles,
crumbs to the girls below.

Like a bronze god
he studies the shore
deciding who will live,
and when to be a hero.

≈Hermit Crab

I find a shell, maybe empty,
but it moves
when I go to pick it up.

A tiny crab emerges: claw,
head, two glittering eyes,
pulling the shell behind.

Two kids come over,
girls older than me,
both wearing bikinis,
their bodies gleaming
with suntan lotion.

He's so cute,
one of them says
bending down to look.

She smells sweet,
like coconut oil,
touches the shell
but it gets spooked
and hides inside.

Her friend smiles at me,
asks: *Can you make it
come out?*

Gotta go, I mumble,
and run to the water.

≈Hanging Out

At high noon I'm sitting
with four of my friends:
sunning, talking, goofing,
just hanging out.

Let's race to the Point
          Nah, let's play football
Let's go get a soda
          You don't got no money
Yeah but you've got a twenty
          so you can hook us all up

Everybody's got an idea
but nobody moves.

The tide is way out,
the sun's beating down,
you can't see a shadow,
and it almost feels like
time has stopped.

≈Wallowing

We walk on our hands
and laze in shallow surf

like a bunch of sea sloths
or slow motion manatees

no place to go
no hurry to get there

wubbling with the bubbles
foaming with the froth

in the noisy crumble tumble
of the ragamuffin waves

≈Beach Baby

She's one year old. One tooth. A total pudge.
She tries to get out of the water but her
soaked diaper must weigh
ten thousand pounds
so all she can do is
sit.

Later she sees me eating Cheese Puffs
and toddles over, towering above me,
a baby so giant she blocks out the sun,
sticks out her hand, and yells: *MINE!*

Her mother hustles over, apologizes,
and hauls her back to their blanket.
The baby starts eating sand, grinning,
grinding the grains with that one tooth.

≈ College Girls

I pass by a pack of girls
each wearing a DUKE cap,
soaking up the last of the sun.

I can't overhear any words,
just the sound of laughing
about who knows what.

I try not to stare at them,
tanned and oiled and sleek,
eyes hidden by dark glasses,

goddesses from another galaxy.

≈Girl Questions

Why would you wear makeup
to a place
        like the beach?

Why do they insist on going
in groups
        to the concession?

Why do they always go to
the restroom
        at the same time?

Why do girls always seem to like
the dumbest
        show-off guys?

≈ Block That Tide!

I'm just goofing around,
digging all by myself,
building a sand wall
against the high tide.

I've made a big mound
when a wave attacks.
A break! Cold water
flooding my ankles.

A kid jumps in yelling:
Put seaweed in the walls!
A girl joins us, then Ben,
now there are four of us

shoulder to shoulder,
screaming like crazy,
running out of time,
digging, desperate,

reinforcing the walls with
shells, seaweed, driftwood,
any weapon we can use
against the attacking waves.

We know it's impossible
but we want a place in
The Guinness Book of World Records:
KIDS WHO BLOCKED THE TIDE

≈ Watching Teenagers

I count six girls
bopping to music,
boogying in the sand.

A muscle-y boy
tries a handstand
but wipes out big time.

One pimply kid throws a girl
kicking and screaming
into the water.

Whatta tough guy!

When I'm a teenager
I'm never
getting zits on my face

and I'm never going to
make a fool of myself
just to impress some girl.

≈ Looking

She looks over
>I look down.

I look over
>she looks away.

She looks over
smiling, waving,
and I smile back
'til I realize she's
waving to some kid
behind me.

Believe me: it's much easier
swapping baseball cards
than trading looks
with a girl.

≈ Can I Use Your Cell Phone?

I spot Ramona Sierra
a girl in my class
hanging with two other girls.

She waves me to come over
so I sort of saunter, real slow,
to their cluster of towels.

They've got music and chips
and legs greased up
with too much lotion.

Ramona squints up and asks:
Can we use your cell phone
to order a pepperoni pizza?

Of course I don't have one
but I grab a broken clamshell
and toss it to her, saying:

Sure, use my shell-ular phone

and the sound of their laughter
erupts
like a flock of startled birds.

≈ Digging

My brother uses a stick
to make a hole in the sand.

> He says: *There's water here*
> *if you dig down deep enough.*

I ignore him, close my eyes,
and just let my thoughts drift.

I liked the way it felt
when I made her laugh.

Wish I could dig down
to more of that sound.

≈ Marooned

I'm burying my feet in wet sand
when Ramona comes over
and plops down beside me.

What would you do if you
got trapped on an island?

> *I'd write a letter*
> *asking for help.*

But what would you
use for a pen?

> *I'd get a feather*
> *from a seagull.*

But how would you make
the letters look dark?

> *I'd use ink*
> *from a squid.*

But what would you
write it on?

> *Dried white seaweed.*

But how would you
mail it?

> *I'd throw it out to sea*
> *in a corked bottle*
> *marked*
> *OCEAN DELIVERY.*

≈ Man with a Metal Detector

He's the kind of guy
people would make fun of:
wearing those bulky earphones,
moving around that weird contraption,
some kind of vacuum
to sniff the scent of gold.

> Mom tells me: *Last year*
> *he lost his wife to cancer.*
> *They were best friends,*
> *married forty years.*

He walks the lonely beach
in an ugly Hawaiian shirt,
eyes shut, concentrating,
listening for the sound
of somebody else's
lost treasure.

≋ Crossroads

In the slanting sunshine
every scrap of seaweed
snaps into perfect focus.

Here at the shoreline
the earth meets sky
and sea meets land.

I stand at the crossroads,
no longer a little kid,
but not yet grown up.

≋ Shadow Football

At first I hardly notice this dark
spirit spilling out of me until

I have a double exactly my size
matching me step for step.

We're playing football, two-on-two,
but it looks more like four-on-four

with all these shadows joining in
tangling long limbs with ours.

Then they detach from our bodies
and start to play their own game!

Tall figures move silently among us
like the ghosts of immortal players.

They honor us with their presence
and show the way to greatness.

≋First Lullaby

In late afternoon
the sea breathes
coolness
onto the shore.

Lying on a towel
I feel the sand
still glowing
with the memory
of the day's hottest sun.

The beach hushes
at this time of day
and it sounds like the
world's first lullaby:
the low throaty waves,
salty breeze in my ears,
and Mom humming.

≈ Staying Lately

When my brother Ben asks:
Can we stay at the beach lately?
he means late and Mom says yes.

Most people come to the beach early,
head home around mid-afternoon
when the sun starts to fade.

Mom says her favorite beach time
is late afternoon
and she gets no argument from me.

Dad will meet us here around six o'clock
bringing food for supper
and we'll have the beach all to ourselves.

≈New Sun

Ragged clouds sweep in
bringing darkness
and rain.

From the concession stand
we watch the angry
splintered sky.

Families sprint for their cars
little kids yowling
clothes soaked through.

The squall tips over barrels
turns umbrellas inside out
blows the rain sideways

plays a crazed game of soccer
with abandoned beach balls
according to its own rules.

But the storm doesn't last:
the clouds lighten
and gulls reclaim the sky.

The sun bursts through
throwing confetti
all over the sea.

This new sun feels like
a present
I didn't expect to get.

≈ Scavengers

By the end of the storm
almost everyone has left.

The sand feels cool and muddy
with a million tiny rain craters.

I hear the low voice of waves
and the raucous sound of birds.

Hundreds of gulls have descended
onto the deserted beach to claim

a bonanza of soggy french fries,
crusts, cookies, apple cores.

The beach will stay empty
except for these birds and us,

happy to scavenge the leftover
scraps from this summer day.

≈ The Last Swimmer

Mom lets us swim forever
but she has one firm rule:
when your lips turn blue
you've got to get out
and warm up.

Ben's teeth are chattering,
his lips are all purplish blue.
He tries to hide it from Mom
but she makes him get out,
folds him into a huge towel,
snuggles him on her lap.

It's way past six o'clock now.
Mr. Lifeguard has abandoned
his perch and gone home.

Nobody else in the water.

I'm the last swimmer
and this is my ocean:
every wave is mine.

≋Great Blue Heron

Even when we walk up close
he pays no attention to us
as he walks along the shore
peering into shallow water
looking for some juicy crab
or unsuspecting sushi.

He looks like a dorky teacher
teaching advanced algebra,
all eyes and bones and beak,
lecturing to invisible students,
hungry for that one moment
when he will get across his

                                point.

≈ Dad

My mouth starts watering
seeing Dad walk toward us
carrying soda and a paper bag.

He buys the world's best subs:
thick sandwiches long as your arm
jam-packed with cheese and meat

dripping with onions and vinegar
but I'm a little worried now when I
don't see them sticking out of his bag.

*Don't worry, he says. I've got hot dogs,
potatoes, cole slaw, graham crackers,
marshmallows, and chocolate bars,*

and a permit for a bonfire.

≋ Sunset

The sun dips
           to its lowest point,
painting the sky in colors you can't
find in any box of crayons.

Magenta goes to extraterrestrial pink
and rays like spun silver introduce
a new kind of light
to the world.

The sun touches the horizon
lighting a brilliant path
from us to our star,
a fiery core of gold.

We stand without speaking,
Dad puts his arms around Mom,
Ben says: *I see my soul, dancing*.

≈Bonfire

Night gathers around us.
We collect dry driftwood
that erupts into flames
when Dad lights the match.

When the fire dies down
Mom tucks four fat potatoes
deep into the blood red coals
and we all wait for supper.

We hear the fire hiss and roar

> *or is that a wave*
> *on the dark ocean?*

We watch a fire spark
hover above us

> *or is that the*
> *night's first star?*

≈Driving Home

Our car is a seashell
in an ocean of darkness.

I'm so tired I can barely
keep both eyes open.

I've got sand in my ears,
hair, shoes, bathing suit.

The drying salt water
makes my skin feel tight

like now it's one size
too small.